A Good Comb

D0933116

A GOOD COMB

The Sayings of Muriel Spark

Edited by Penelope Jardine

A NEW DIRECTIONS
PAPERBOOK ORIGINAL

Copyright © 2018 Copyright Administration Limited
Preface copyright © 2018 by Penelope Jardine

All rights reserved. Except for brief passages quoted in a
newspaper, magazine, radio, television, or website review,
no part of this book may be reproduced in any form or by
any means, electronic or mechanical, including photo-
copying and recording, or by any information storage and
retrieval system, without permission in writing from the
Publisher.

Published by arrangement with Georges Borchardt, Inc.,
New York.

Manufactured in the United States of America
New Directions Books are printed on acid-free paper.
First published as a New Directions Paperbook Original
in 2018

Library of Congress Cataloging-in-Publication Data
Names: Spark, Muriel author. | Jardine, Penelope editor.
Title: A good comb : the sayings of Muriel Spark /
edited by Penelope Jardine.
Description: New York : New Directions Books, 2018.
Identifiers: LCCN 2017041787 | ISBN 9780811227605
(alk. paper)
Subjects: LCSH: Spark, Muriel--Quotations.
Classification: LCC PR6037.P29 A6 2018 |
DDC 828/.91402—dc23
LC record available at https://lccn.loc.gov/2017041787

10 9 8 7 6 5 4 3 2 1

New Directions Books are published for James Laughlin
by New Directions Publishing Corporation
80 Eighth Avenue, New York 10011

A Good Comb

is dedicated to its author

MURIEL SPARK

on the centenary of her birth

FEBRUARY 1, 1918

with love and affection

from her publisher and editor

Contents

Preface

It should be said at once that the contents of this selection should not be taken too seriously. This is FICTION after all. The words are not gospel of what Muriel Spark was thinking or wishing to say, only that in the context of a story the character would very likely have said this. That doesn't mean that Dame Muriel did not actually think what she says here, and perhaps she meant it very much. But above all, the words found here are certainly meant to entertain. Entertainment was a big part of her creative process. She didn't like moaning people, neither did she moan herself. She was a comic of serious intent.

For Muriel, a meal in a restaurant meant the food and drink were only secondary to a wonderful snippet of conversation overheard at the next table and stored away for the novel in hand; such as, "There's a wealth of wild flowers and butterflies" from the English abroad, overheard in Tuscany, and to be found in *A Far Cry from Kensington*.

There was also the Observing Eye. Muriel was aware of people nearby, who, crossing their legs in a chair, more or less unconsciously put a foot in your mouth. You will find wisdom in these Sayings, coming from an exceptional observer: She of the "X-ray eyes," as Shirley Hazzard noted. See how many gifts to writers are here of Muriel's lifetime experience in her craft.

These Sayings are full of advice, designed to make you laugh from their unexpected resolutions and to make you think as you take in some outrageous thoughts. However it is all in a fictional setting so do not be too upset. Withstand! They are devastating.

The idea for this book was probably inspired by an edition of Kafka's *Aphorisms,* sent to Muriel by the Italian publisher Roberto Calasso. Muriel was impressed by a Saying of Kafka's: "A cage goes in search of a bird." She thought it summed up perfectly Martin Stannard's biography of her, as he completely missed catching her essence in his book despite reams and reams of scholarly research. "Brevity," we are told, "is the Soul of Wit." Muriel followed this maxim to the letter. Some Sayings spring open, like the traps beneath hanged men.

Finally, my rough extraction of these Sayings has been put into shape by Barbara Epler of this very creative and invaluable publishing house. I am enormously grateful to her for this intelligent arrangement.

PENELOPE JARDINE

A Few Words of Advice

An old and famous actress had once given her the following advice: If you must make any excuse make one only. More than one sounds false. None at all is best. It's generally foolish to make excuses and give reasons. Never try to explain yourself to others, it leads to confusion. Avoid psychiatrists.

There's nothing like work to calm your emotions.

If you choose the sort of life which has no conventional pattern you have to try to make an art of it, or it is a mess.

I have always been free with advice; but it is one thing to hand out advice and another to persuade people to accept it.

Enough is always enough.

"For concentration," I said, "you need a cat. Do you happen to have a cat?"

So I passed him some very good advice that if you want to concentrate deeply on some problem, you should acquire a cat. Alone with the cat in the room where you work, I explained, the cat will invariably get up on your desk and settle placidly under the desk-lamp. The light from the lamp, I explained, gives a cat great satisfaction. The cat will settle down and be serene, with a serenity that passes all understanding. And the tranquility of the cat will gradually come to affect you, sitting there at your desk, so that all the excitable qualities that impede your concentration compose themselves and give your mind back the self-command it has lost. You need not watch the cat all the time. Its presence alone is enough. The effect of a cat on your concentration is remarkable, very mysterious.

She decided, therefore, essentially "I am who I am" was indeed the final definition for her.

And now a word about good manners. If it can be said of you that you've got "exquisite manners," it's deadly. Almost as bad as having a name for being rude. Ostentatious manners, like everything else showy, are terribly bad. If you're a man don't bow and scrape. Never wash your hands in the air as did a late Cardinal on my acquaintance, when trying to please someone. If you're a girl, just show a lot of consideration to the elderly. There's no need to jump to your feet if one of your friend's parents comes into the room, far less your own. It looks too well trained. Try not to look very well brought up, it's awful. At the same time, you should consider others round you. Don't be boring as so many people are, who have exquisite manners. Never behave as if people didn't exist.

Any correspondence that's bloody boring, just pull the chain on it.

People should definitely not quote the Scriptures at each other.

Any system which doesn't allow for the unexpected and the unwelcome is a rotten one.

It was in those days of the early fifties of this century that I formed the habit of insomnia. Insomnia is not bad in itself. You can lie awake at night and think; the quality of insomnia depends entirely on what you decide to think of. Can you decide to think?—Yes, you can. You can put your mind to anything most of the time.

At night I lay awake looking at the darkness, listening to the silence, prefiguring the future, picking out of the past the scraps I had overlooked, those rejected events which now came to the foreground, large and important, so that the weight of destiny no longer bore on the current problems of my life, whatever they were at the time (for who lives without problems every day? Why waste the nights on them?)

Beware the wickedness of the righteous.

It is my advice to any woman getting married to start, not as you mean to go on, but worse, tougher, than you mean to go on. Then you can slowly relax and it comes as a pleasant surprise.

Discretion is always desirable.

Children are quite psychic ... Very intuitive. They can tune into your thoughts, it's a bit disquieting. You should try always to give them happy memories. It's the only thing you can leave to your children with any certainty — happy memories.

It is a good thing to go to Paris for a few days if you have had a lot of trouble, and that is my advice to everyone except Parisians.

How like the death wish is to the life-urge! How urgently does an overwhelming obsession with life lead to suicide! Really, it's best to be half-awake and half-aware. That is the happiest stage.

If you look for one thing, you frequently find another.

Be gentle. It is beautiful to be gentle with those who suffer. There is no beauty in the world so great as beauty of action. It stands, contained in its own moment, from everlasting to everlasting.

It is well, when in difficulties, to say never a word, neither black nor white. Speech is silver but silence is golden.

Now, it is my advice to anyone getting married, that they should first see the other partner when drunk. Especially a man. Drink can mellow, it can sweeten. Too much can make a person silly. Or it can make them a savage.

Beware of men bearing flowers.

Love takes time.

Things mount up inside one, and then one has to perpetrate an outrage.

I can tell you that if there's nothing wrong with you except fat it is easy to get thin. You eat and drink the same as always, only half. If you are handed a plate of food, leave half; if you have to help yourself, take half. After a while, if you are a perfectionist, you can consume half of that again.

I must say that without trying, nobody gets any-thing, anywhere.

Writing

I've come to learn for myself how little one needs, in the art of writing, to convey the lot, and how a lot of words, on the other hand, can convey so little.

No matter what is described it seems to me a sort of hypocrisy for a writer to pretend to be undergoing tragic experiences when obviously one is sitting in relative comfort with a pen and paper or before a typewriter.

The novel took up the sweetest part of my mind and the rarest part of my imagination; it was like being in love only better.

I may take up detective work one of these days. It would be quite my sort of thing.

Sometimes I don't actually meet a character I have created in a novel until some time after the novel has been written and published.

The main thing about a story is that it should end well, and perhaps it is not too much to say that a story's ending casts its voice, color, tone and shade over the whole work.

I see no reason to keep silent about my enjoyment of the sound of my own voice as I work.

Since the story of my own life is just as much constituted of the secrets of my craft as it is of other events, I might as well remark here that to make a character ring true it needs to, must be in some way, contradictory, somewhere a paradox.

Now, it fell to me to give advice to many authors which in at least two cases bore fruit. So I will repeat it here, free of charge. It proved helpful to the type of writer who has some imagination and wants to write a novel but doesn't know how to start.

"You are writing a letter to a friend," was the sort of thing I used to say. "And this is a dear and close friend, real—or better—invented in your mind like a fixation. Write privately, not publicly; without fear or timidity, right to the end of the letter, as if it was never going to be published, so that your true friend will read it over and over, and then want more enchanting letters from you. Now, you are not writing about the relationship between your friend and yourself; you take that for granted. You are only confiding an experience that you think only he will enjoy reading. What you have to say will come out more spontaneously and honestly than if you are thinking of numerous readers. Before starting the letter rehearse in your mind what you are going to tell; something interesting, your story. But don't rehearse too much, the story will develop as you go along, especially if you write to a special friend, man or woman, to make them smile or laugh or cry, or anything you like so long as you know it will interest. Remember not to think of the reading public, it will put you off."

I suppose, as a novelist, I should welcome any experience. Of course, a novelist doesn't really have to undergo every experience, a glimpse is enough.

I think a stylish life is unsuitable to the writer, and very often in the house where there's a mild disorder one finds the writer with the best powers of organizing his work. Order where order is due.

"Couldn't you talk to him about your work, you know?"

"Oh, God, Carmelita. It would be easier to write the bloody essay myself."

He congratulated me on my piece of luck. He said, "Of course, a popular success ..." and didn't finish the sentence. He said, "Well, I'll always be your friend," as if I were out on bail.

She wondered if this was how Father felt in his great depressions when he sat all day, staring and enduring, and all night miraculously wrote the ache out of his system in prose of harsh merriment.

[My novel], shoved quickly out of sight when my visitors arrived, or lest the daily woman should clean it up when I left home in the morning for my job, took up the sweetest part of my mind and the rarest part of my imagination; it was like being in love and better. All day long when I was busy with the affairs of the Autobiographical Association, I had my unfinished novel personified almost as a secret companion and accomplice following me like a shadow wherever I went, whatever I did. I took no notes, except in my mind.

I didn't know then, as I know now, that the traditional paranoia of authors is nothing compared to the inalienable schizophrenia of publishers.

"Sometimes I got tired of being called lucky by everybody. There were times when, privately practicing my writing about life, I knew the bitter side of my fortune. When I failed again and again to reproduce life in some satisfactory and perfect form, I was the more imprisoned, for all my carefree living, within my craving for this satisfaction. Sometimes, in my impotence and need I secreted a venom which infected all of my life for days on end and which spurted out indiscriminately on Skinny or on anyone who crossed my path."

I was going about my proper business, eating my supper while listening-in to the conversation at the next table. One of them said, "There we were all gathered in the living-room, waiting for him." It was all I needed. That was the start of *Warrender Chase*, the first chapter. All the rest sprang from the phrase.

Without a mythology, a novel is nothing. The true novelist, one who understands the work as a continuous poem, is a myth maker, and the wonder of the art resides in the endless different ways of telling a story, and the methods are mythological by nature.

I would write about them one day. In fact, under one form or another, whether I have liked it or not, I have written about them ever since, the straws from which I have made my bricks.

Characters don't live their own lives ... they live the lives I give them ... I'm in full control ... I never thought they could have another life but what I provide on the typed page. Perhaps the readers, later on, will absorb them in an extended imagination, but I don't. Nobody in my book so far could cross the road unless I make them do it.

It was a long time ago. I've been writing ever since with great care. I always hope the readers of my novels are of good quality. I wouldn't like to think of anyone cheap reading my books.

Sex & Love

It is impossible to repent of love. The sin of love does not exist.

She was surprised by a reawakening of that same buoyant and airy discovery of sex, a total sensation which it was impossible to say was physical or mental, only that it contained the lost guileless delight of her eleventh year.... There was nothing whatever to be done about it, but the concise happening filled her with astonishment whenever it came to mind in later days and with a sense of the hidden possibilities in all things.

"Look," she said, "just because I go to bed with a man isn't to say I'm going to rub shoulders with him."

The subject was no more mentioned, save as passed on from fathers to sons, mothers to daughters, like the local genealogies, the infallible methods of shooting to kill, and the facts of life.

Either religious faith penetrates everything in life or it doesn't. There are some experiences that seem to make nonsense of all separations of sacred from profane—they seem childish. Either the whole of life is unified under God or everything falls apart. Sex is child's play in the argument.

Sex is child's play. Jesus Christ was very sophisticated on the subject of sex. And didn't harp on it. Why is it so predominant and serious for us? There are more serious things in the world. And if sex is not child's play, in any case it is worthless. For she was thinking of her own recent experiences of sex, which were the only experiences she knew that were worth thinking about. It was child's play, unselfconscious and so full of fun and therefore of peace, that she had not bothered to analyze or define it. And, she thought, we have invented sex guilt to take our minds off the real thing.

The Castlemaine idea wasn't enough, after all. You can't go to bed with an idea.

Maisie looked remarkably like her rival, as do so many women whose men cannot really escape from them, but seek the same person in other arms.

I couldn't have gone over the border with him. Perhaps forever. Neither my temperament nor my temperature would stand it.

Grandmothers, great-grandfathers, and all antecedents. Don't forget they lived ordinary lives, had pains, went to work, talked, busied themselves, had sex—Full days and full nights, as long as all that lasted. I see no reason to drool over them. They did not drool over us. They thought, if they wanted and could, of the future, the generations to come, but only in the most general terms, obviously, in the nature of things.

There was altogether too much candor in married life; it was an indelicate modern idea, and frequently led to upsets in a household, if not divorce.

"Put your arms around her," he said, becoming a lady-columnist, "and start afresh. It frequently needs but one little gesture from one partner—"

You can't allow for funny passions in a girl that isn't beautiful.

Certainly, you can analyze it and expound its various senses and intentions, but there is always something left over, mysteriously hovering between music and meaning.

And it was always to be the same. Later, when she was famous for sex, her magnificently appealing qualities lay in the fact that she had no curiosity about sex at all, she never reflected upon it. As Miss Brodie was to say, she had instinct.

How can she truly love? She's too timid to hate well, let alone love. It takes courage to practice love.

He was put off her sexually by the thought of her being a spiritualist.

Literary men, if they like women at all, do not want literary women but girls.

And they made love like foreigners, which was alright, too.

"Sex is normal" he says, "I'm cured. Sex is all right."

"It's all right at the time and it's all right before," says Lise, "but the problem is afterwards. That is, if you aren't just an animal. Most of the time, afterwards is pretty sad."

He didn't do his own cooking or press his own trousers. Why should he have consorted, excuse my language with his own wife?

"Sex," she says, "is a subject like any other subject. Every bit as interesting as agriculture."

Why should they trouble themselves about a sa-
lacious nun and a Jesuit? I must say a Jesuit, or
any priest for that matter, would be the last man
I would myself elect to be laid by. A man who
undresses, maybe; but one who unfrocks, no.

Her strength resides in her virginity of heart
combined with the long education of her youth
that took her across many an English quad by
night, across many a campus of Europe and
so to bed. A wealthy woman, more than most,
she has always maintained, is likely to remain
virgin at heart. Her past lovers had been the
most learned available; however ungainly, it was
invariably the professors, the more profound
scholars, who attracted her. And she always felt
learned herself, thereafter by kind of osmosis.

How seldom one falls in love with the lovable
… How seldom … Hardly ever. How do you
know when you're in love? The traffic in the city
improves and the cost of living seems to be very
low.

"The vows of marriage," says he, "are mostly made under the influence of love-passion. I am talking of modern marriages where the partners have been free to choose for themselves. They are in love. I am not talking about arranged marriages where the parents, the families, have combined to bring the union. Good. We have a love-match. Let me tell you," says Hurley, "that the vows of love-passion are like confessions obtained under torture. Erotic love is a madness. Neither of the partners know what they are doing, saying. They are in extremis. The vows of love-passion should at least be liable to be discounted. That is why it is possible, and in fact imperative, for a Catholic, who is supposed to belong to the most rational religion, to believe in divorce between people who have been in love, the marriage vows being made in a state of mental imbalance, which amorous love is. There is a reservation, under Catholic laws of annulment, that allows for madness."

"If I were to impart to you the erotic details of what goes on in my mind they would excite you but per se would consequently cease to excite me."

I have noticed that people in love and having a love affair are more aware of the sexual potential in others than those who are not.

Not having a lover myself at the time, I saw and I didn't see.

Wisdom

One learns to accept oneself.

Snobs are really amazing. They mainly err in failing to fool the very set of people they are hoping to be accepted by, and above all, to seem to belong to, to be taken for. They may live in a democratic society—it does nothing to help, nothing.

Being over seventy is like being engaged in a war. All our friends are going or gone and we survive amongst the dead and dying as on a battlefield.

Impossible to admit evidence in connection with a crime too unspeakable to speak about.

These thoughts overwhelmed Mrs. Pettigrew with that sense of having done a foolish thing against one's interests, which in some people stands for guilt.

When misfortune occurs to slightly absurd or mean-minded people it is indeed tragic for them—it falls with a thud which they don't expect; it does not excite the pity and fear of the onlooker, it excites the revulsion more likely; so that the piece of bad luck which happened ... was not truly tragic, only pathetic.

I haven't changed at all so far as I still think charming friends need not possess minds.

Ridicule is the only honorable weapon we have left.

"We could make changes in government, and later we could change the desert wastes and the sky even, if we could first make changes in ourselves."

Reality, however, refuses to accommodate the idealist.

I was into my fifties, and getting old. How nerve-wracking it is to be getting old, how much better to be old!

Henry Mortimer, the former Chief Inspector, was long, lean, bald and spritely. At the sides and back of his head his hair grew thick and grey. His eyebrows were thick and black. It would be accurate to say that his nose and lips were thick, his eyes small and his chin receding into his neck. And yet it would be inaccurate to say he was not a handsome man, such being the power of unity when it exists in a face.

"I am an honest man ... when treating of the few existing subjects to which honesty is due."

He ruminated on the question why scientific observation differed from humane observation, and the same people, observed in these respective senses, actually seemed to be different people.

"Oh, what people say! They always look at what might be, or what should be, never at what is."

All women under the sun are unscrupulous if there's something they want.

A vision of evil may be as effective to conversion as a vision of good.

It was one's duty in life to be agreeable.

A very boring guest or a very entertaining one could provoke all sorts of undesirable feelings in people.

Death is that sort of thing you can't sleep off.

He was endowed also with that gift which some men keep furtively out of sight like a family skeleton, an inward court of appeal with powers to reverse all varieties of mental verdicts.

If it were only true that all's well that ends well, if only it were true.

It's an extraordinary fact ... that just at the precise moment when you're at your wits' end it's always the last people in the world you want to see who turn up, full of themselves, demanding total attention. It's always the exceptionally tiresome who barge in at the exceptionally difficult moment.

It is a common misunderstanding that one who does not know another's mother tongue is assumed to be less intelligent and discerning than he is.

Philosophers, when they cease philosophizing and take up action, are dangerous. Then why ask her advice? Because we are in danger. Dangerous people understand well how to avoid it.

What did it matter if they knew what he might be up to, and he knew that they knew, since, if he put his mind to it he could easily make as many accurate guesses about their doings as they could about his.

She always made her own environment. She seemed to rule Nature, more and more as she got older.

It had been that situation where the visitor who came to stay remained to live.

Suffering isn't in proportion to what the sufferer deserves.

Suicide is something we know too little about, simply because the chief witness has died, frequently with his secret that no suicide-note seems adequate to square with the proportions of the event.

"She has evolved a theory that people are psychologically of a certain era. 'Some people,' she now informs Brian, 'are eighteenth century, some fifteenth, some third century, some twentieth. All practicing psychiatrists should be students of history. Most patients are blocked,' she says, 'in their historical era and cannot cope with the claims and habits of our century.'"

Providers are often disliked, often despised.

I think "waiter" is such a funny word. It is we who wait.

"If there's anything I can't stand it's a love-hate relationship ... The element of love in such a relation simply isn't worthy of the name. It boils down to hatred pure and simple in the end. Love comprises among other things a desire for the well-being and spiritual freedom of the one who is loved. There's an objective quality about love. Love-hate is obsessive, it is possessive. It can be evil in effect."

One thing that the Book of Job teaches us ...
is the futility of friendship in times of trouble.
That is perhaps not a reflection on friends but
on friendship. Friends mean well, or make as if
they do. But friendship itself is made for happi-
ness, not trouble.

Everyone likes to be on the winning side.

It calms you down, a good comb.

Religion

I thought him a charming and witty character with a ready answer, and with a lot of conflicting sides to his nature. I liked God.

The beautiful and dangerous gift of faith, which, by definition of the Scriptures, is the sum of things hoped for and the evidence of things unseen.

The True Church was awful, though unfortunately, one couldn't deny, true.

Everyone gives to the poor; they try to save their souls by it. But if a poor man gives to the rich, his soul is already with God, and the souls of the rich are mysteriously moved and relieved of a burden.

The demands of the Christian religion are exorbitant, they are outrageous. Christians who don't realize that from the start are not faithful. They are dishonest; their teachers are talking in their sleep. "Love one another ... brethren, brethren ... your brother, neighbors, love, love, love"—do they know what they are saying?

It is possible for a man matured in religion by half a century of punctilious observance, having advanced himself in devotion the slow and exquisite way, trustfully ascending his winding stair, and, to make assurance doubly sure, supplementing his meditations by deep-breathing exercises twice daily, to go into a flat spin when faced with some trouble which does not come within a familiar category. Should this occur, it causes dismay in others. To anyone accustomed to respect the wisdom and control of a contemplative creature, the evidence of his failure to cope with a normal emergency is distressing. Only the spiritual extremists rejoice—the Devil on account of his crude triumph, and the very holy souls because they discern in such behavior a testimony to the truth that human nature is apt to fail in spite of regular prayer and deep breathing.

"To them, it was no great shock when I turned Catholic, since with Roman Catholics too, it all boils down to the Almighty in the end."

It was a humiliating thought, which in turn was good for the soul.

"A good death," she said, "doesn't reside in the dignity of bearing but in the disposition of the soul."

In some ways the most real and rooted people made no evasions about their belief that God had planned for practically everybody before they were born a nasty surprise when they died: [it was] God's pleasure to implant in certain people an erroneous sense of joy and salvation, so that their surprise at the end might be the nastier.

That Catholic habit of belittling what was secretly feared.

Being a Jew isn't something they consider in their minds, weigh up, and give assent as one does in the Western Christian tradition. Being a Jew is inherent.

One could prove anything against anyone from the Bible.

A woman who had embraced the Catholic Church instead of a husband, one who had taken up religion instead of cats.

How it was possible to do things for their own sake, not only possible but sometimes necessary for the affirmation of one's personal identity. The ideal reposed in their religion, but somewhere in the long trail of Islam, the knack of disinterestedness had been lost, and with it a large portion of the joy of life.

The act of pilgrimage is an instinct of mankind. It is an act of devotion, which, like a work of art, is meaning enough in itself. The questions, "What useful purpose does a pilgrimage serve? What good does it do?" are by the way. People put themselves out to visit places sacred to their religion, or the graves of poets and statesmen, or of their ancestors, or the house they themselves were born in. Why? Because that is what people do.

Doubt is the prerogative of the believer; the unbeliever cannot know doubt. And in what is doubtful we should doubt well. But in whatever touches the human spirit, it is better to believe everything than nothing.

"I smell an ideology, that's all."

"She claims a special enlightenment. Felicity wants everyone to be liberated by her vision and to acknowledge it. She wants a stamped receipt from the Almighty God for every word she spends, every action, as if she can later deduct it from her income-tax returns. Felicity will never see the point of faith unless it visibly benefits mankind. She is bent on helping lame dogs over stiles. Then they can't get back over again to limp home."

Their religious apprehensions were different from mine. "Different from" is the form my neurosis took. I do like the differentiation of things, but it is apt to lead to nerve-wracking pursuits. On the other hand, life led on the different-from level is always an adventure.

"We are all the same," she would assert, infuriating me because I knew that God had made everyone unique. "We are all the same" was her way of saying we were all equal in the sight of God. Still, the inaccuracy irritated me.

There was a time I greatly desired not to believe, but I found myself at last unable not to believe.

I enjoy a puritanical and moralistic nature; it is my happy element to judge between right and wrong, regardless of what I might actually do. At the same time, the wreaking of vengeance and imposing of justice on others and myself are not at all in my line. It is enough for me to discriminate mentally and leave the rest to God.

The Pope should broaden his ecumenical views and he ought to stand by the Second Vatican Council. He should throw the dogmas out of the window there at the Holy See and he ought to let the other religions in by the door and unite.

Cherished hate is a great evil, anyway.

Like ministers of any other religion, he was estranged from reality in proportion as he mistook the nature of prayer, offering up his words of praise, of gratitude, penitence, intercession and urgent petition in the satisfaction that his god would reply in kind, hear, smile, and wave a wand.

She seemed embarrassed to be there, as if the place was a pawnshop or a Roman Catholic confessional which one might be seen going into or coming out of.

I've never held it right to create more difficulties in matters of religion than already exist.

For he could not face that a benevolent Creator, one whose charming and delicious light descended and spread over the world, and being powerful everywhere, could condone the unspeakable sufferings of the world; that God did permit all suffering and was therefore, by logic of his omnipotence, the actual author of it, he was at a loss how to square with the existence of God, given the premise that God is good.

"It is the only problem … It's the only problem, in fact, worth discussing."

Our limitations of knowledge make us puzzle over the cause of suffering, maybe it is the cause of suffering itself … As I say, we are plonked here in the world and nobody but our own kind can tell us anything. It isn't enough. As for the rest, God doesn't tell.

A good disposition is more precious to God than fine feelings.

The more religious people are, the more perplexing I find them.

Art

What is truth? When people say that nothing happens in their lives I believe them. But you must understand that everything happens to an artist; time is always redeemed, nothing is lost and wonders never cease.

I would far rather have a present of a good story than, say, a bunch of flowers, and will more or less always take kindly to the raconteur type.

The eye of the true artist doesn't see life in the way of goods paid for. The world is ours. It is our birthright. We take it without payment.

The greatest literature is the occasional kind, a mere after-thought.

What are scenarios? ... They are an art-form, ... based on facts. A good scenario is a garble. A bad one is a bungle. They need not be plausible, only hypnotic, like all good art.

They are my own secret rules but they arise from deep conviction. They cannot be formulated, they are as sincere and indescribable as are the primary colors; they are not of a science but of an art.

"Yes," I said, "because I never have scruples about artistic lies."

For one who demands much of life, there is always a certain amount of experience to be discarded as soon as one discovers its fruitlessness.

I am addicted to a form of snobbery which will hardly keep a first edition on its shelves.

The sins of the artist are sins of omission.

She added, "Art is greater than science. Art comes first, and then Science."

To these her mind always came round at length, as in a concerto when the formal recapitulation, the real thing wins through.

She held as a vital principle that the human mind was bound in duty to continuous acts of definition.

What I call midnight oil literature is only done by hand. It's an art.

It isn't what you look, for an artist, it's what you do. . . . You know, when a woman is an artist, she is an artist in many other ways than in practicing the actual art.

I had known for a long time that success could not be my profession in life, nor failure a calling for that matter. These were by-products.

I have never known an artist who at some time in his life has not come into conflict with pure evil, realized as it may have been under the form of disease, injustice, fear, oppression or any other ill element that can afflict living creatures. The reverse doesn't hold: that is to say, it isn't only the artist who suffers, or who perceives evil. But I think it true that no artist has lived who has not experienced and then recognized something at first too incredibly evil to seem real, then so undoubtedly real as to be undoubtedly true.

"They are talking about this artist character's retiring," said Hurley. "All wrong. Artists don't retire. There's nothing for them to retire about."

"My film is not replaceable," said Tom. "No work of art can be replaced. A work of art is like living people."

I would have laid down my conviction that complete frankness is not a quality that favors art.

"But acting is an art that you cannot really learn. A certain amount of training might improve the actor's art, but essentially to be an actor you have to born with the whole stock and merchandise built-in. Acting is fundamentally the art of hypocrisy. Nothing can put it there ... An art is something you bring with you into the world."

Art is an act of daring.

The Observing Eye

"He looked as if he would murder me and he did."

It is not because we are rats that we tend to abandon people who are down, it is because we are embarrassed.

He's buried in his friends' memory. Isn't that enough?

I was fascinated by her rhetoric ... This meaningless coinage, "look at it from a human point of view," as if I were another species, must either be put on for my benefit, in which case she had miscalculated my intelligence, or she herself was under some emotional strain; and I had noticed before, once or twice in my job, that the most intelligent and sophisticated of writers are often banal and incoherent under an emotional pressure of real life. I decided to sip my gin and tonic and let her continue.

The essential thing about herself remained unspoken, uncategorized and unallocated.

There was a heatwave so fierce you would have thought someone had turned it on somewhere by means of a tap, and had turned it too high, and then gone away for the summer.

The father smiled with a curious histrionic glitter of the eye, by which many modern Arabs intended to express proud loathing; they had got the trick from the cinema, over the years.

"Already I felt free of the embarrassing couple. In a curious way Mme. Dessain had released me. She had held out a straw. I clutched it and miraculously it held me up. It struck me she was highly intuitive, as indeed are so many in the hotel business."

A Venetian funeral is intended not to be missed. Even the motor of the barge chugs with mournful dignity. After all this is reflected in the water beneath it: the stately merchandise and arrogance of Venetian death, as of old, when money was weighty and haste was vile.

Usually neurotics take against people whose nerves they can't jar upon.

"He sees already the gleaming buttons of the policemen's uniforms, hears the cold and the confiding, the hot and the barking voices, sees already the holsters and epaulets and all those trappings devised to protect them from the indecent exposure of fear and pity, pity and fear."

It is not that I judge people by their appearance, but it is true that I am fascinated by their faces. I do not stare in their presence. I like to take the impression of a face home with me, there to stare at and chew over it in privacy, as a wild beast prefers to devour its prey in concealment.

As a means of judging character it is a misleading practice and as for physiognomy the science, I know nothing of that. The misleading element, in fact, provides the essence of my satisfaction. In the course of deciphering a face, its shape, tones, lines and droops as if these were words and sentences of a message from the interior, I fix upon it a character which, though I know it to be distorted, never quite untrue, never entirely true, interests me. I am as near the mark as myth is to history, the apocrypha to the canon.

To a delicate ear her tone might have resembled the stab of a pin stuck into a waxen image.

I had the rare and distressing experience of becoming objectively conscious of my rational mind in action, separate from all others, as one might see the open workings of a clock. This only happens to me when faced with a group of facts which hurt my reasoning powers—as one becomes highly conscious of a limb when it is damaged.

Marion stooped and took a cake as if it was her last chance of ever eating a cake again.

She was, of course, as a follower of Lenin, class-conscious by profession.

"Money, money, you are always talking about money. Let us run up debts. One is nobody without debts."

The nicest boy who ever committed the sin of whisky.

She was astonishingly ugly, one was compelled to look at her.

She desires the ecstasy of murdering me in some prolonged ritualistic orgy; she sees I am grisly about the truth; she sees I am well-dressed and good-looking. Perhaps she senses my weakness, my loathing of human flesh where the bulk outweighs the intelligence.

Her words depressed him. They were like spilt sugar; however much you swept it up some grain would keep grinding under your feet.

She ate steadily on as one who proves, by eating on during another's distress, the unshakable sanity of their advice.

"I'm passionate about justice. Like all the Irish."

He touched her arm consolingly as a man of integrity to a woman who could not be expected to understand integrity.

He said, as one who keeps the conversation flowing, not withstanding a tiger in the garden.

She could converse seriously for hours on a subject, the absence of any wit in her talk having the compensatory value of keeping the main topic in line, without any of the far-flung diversions that humor leads to.

He exhausted his capacity for conversation when he became an Englishman.

He had regained some lost or forgotten element in his nature and was now, at last, for some reason, flowering in the full irrational norm of the stock she also derived from: unselfquestioning hierarchists, anarchistic imperialists, blood-sporting zoophiles, skeptical believers— the whole paradoxical lark that had secured, among their bones, the sane life for the dead generations of British Islanders.

She's suffering from fear, quite a thrilling emotion ... People love it.

"What does it matter if he understands what we say, since we never say anything that matters?"

The English abroad are so awful and they always bring their own life with them. I mean, what's the use of going abroad if you don't get new life from it?

In her whine of bewilderment, that voice of the very stupid, the mind where no dawn breaks.

"Why? is a fastidious question at any time, — when applied to any action of Winifrede's the word 'why' is the inscrutable ingredient of a brown stew.... "

A lady is free; but a Bourgeoise is never free from the desire for freedom.

The look of curiosity which comes over the faces of people to whom nothing much happens, and which, to people of more elaborate lives, looks like hostility.

He thought, in fact, that he exercised a quality which he called style, but was in reality an aggressive cynicism. Style, in the sense that he believed himself to possess it, needs a certain basic humility; and without it there can never be any distinction of manner or of anything whatsoever.

"God and public opinion will judge," Anthea said, as if the two were one and the same.

It was not that he regretted imposing his presence, but that by doing so he must impose the absence to follow.

Job's tragedy was that of the happy ending.

"It may seem far-fetched to you, Anthea, but here everything is stark realism. This is Italy."

"Sandwiches," she said, "like diamonds are forever. Children love them. They are the most useful, yet often the most despised of foods."

It was after two in the morning before I got to bed. I remember how the doings of my day appeared again before me, rich with inexplicable life. I fell asleep with a strange sense of sadness and promise meeting and holding hands.

Power

All of the young of the human species are born omniscient. Babies, in their waking hours, know everything that is going on everywhere in the world; they can tune in to any conversation they choose, switch on to any scene. We have all experienced this power.

She became a tall lighthouse sending out kindly beams which some took for welcome instead of warnings against the rocks.

I had learned over the years that the more you discourage your prospective clients the more they want your work, and the higher the price they are prepared to pay.

She was very old but by no means infirm, especially of purpose.

"As I have said, it isn't easy to give evidence against a child of five. And especially to its mother."

"Dark glasses hide dark thoughts," I said.
  "Is that a saying?"
  "Not that I've heard. But it is one now."

It was only gradually that her importance was permitted to dawn upon strangers.

Freddy kept pace with him from the shadows, not for one wild moment doubting the success of their plan, conceived as it had been in an hour of genius and of brotherhood; all was perfectly feasible, or as good as done, and he walked in that dispensation of mind in which impossible works are in fact accomplished and mountains are moved.

I saw a landowner's recognition in her little black eyes.

"You're mistaken if you think wrong-doers are always unhappy," Grace said. "The really professional evil-doers love it. They're as happy as larks in the sky.... The unhappy ones are only the guilty amateurs and the neurotics," said Grace. "The pros are in their element."

It was, I thought, always desirable that justice should be done. It was one thing to applaud justice, another to bring it about ... I was just as anxious to prevent injustice as to cause justice.

I like to be in a position to choose, I like to be in control of my relationships with people.

But Frau Lublonitsch was a church unto herself, and even resembled in shape the onion-shaped spires of the churches round her.

"I deny there's anything particularly vulgar about money."

The law doesn't like blackmail.

"It's only possible to betray where loyalty is due," said Sandy.

He arranged everything as precisely as a practiced incendiary.

"What is personality but the effect one has on others? Life is all the achievement of an effect. Only the animals remain natural." He told her that personality was different from a person's character, but even character could change over the years, depending on the habits one practiced. "I see no hypocrisy in living up to what the public thinks of you," he said.

Mysterious and intangible, money of Maggie's sort was able to take lightning trips round the world without ever packing its bags or booking its seat on a plane. Indeed, money of any sort is, in reality, unspendable and unwasteable; it can only pass hands wisely or unwisely, or else by means of violence, and, colorless, odorless, and tasteless, it is a token for the colors, smells and savors, for food and shelter and clothing and for representations of beauty, however beauty may be defined by the person who buys it. Only in appearances does money multiply itself; in reality it multiplies the human race, so that even money lavished on funerals is not wasted, neither directly nor indirectly, since it nourishes the undertaker's children's children as the body fertilizes the earth.

The new world which is arising out of the ashes of the old, avid for immaterialism, had begun to sprout forth its responsive worshippers.

"And there's a way of willing people to be serviceable," said Greta. "You can use your willpower and make what is not so, so. Everyone knows that."

With her assistant, Margaret was casual, even scornful: a sure way of eliciting more insistent information.

"What do they think a film set is? A democracy or something?"

"Personally, I think he's evil."

"So do I," Curran said, "and infantile. Which amounts to the same thing when you add a little power. Only a little power."

Truth

To me truth has airy properties with buoyant and lyrical effects; and when anything drastic starts up from some light cause it only proves to me that something false has got into the world.

It is impossible to persuade a man who does not disagree, but smiles.

Laughter. That's what the human race was made for.

Most people took a man, in all respects, for what he said he was.

She did not know then that the price of allowing false opinions was the gradual loss of one's
capacity for forming true ones.

I do not care to go about with nothing on my face
so that everyone can see what is written on it.

There is no more beautiful a sight, he said, than
to see a fine woman bashing away at a typewriter.

"We're very much in love with each other,"
Barry explains, squeezing his wife. And Sybil
wonders what is wrong with their marriage
since obviously something is wrong.

The season of falsity had formed a scab soon
to fall away altogether. There is no health, she
thought, for me, outside of honesty.

"You mustn't think that because I take my gifts
seriously, I take them solemnly. It is all an airy
dream of mine, unsinkable because it is light. I
don't play the eerie fortune-teller at all; I don't
play anything when I play the cards; I am simply
myself."

The sacrifice of pleasure is of course itself a pleasure.

She wasn't a person to whom things happen.

Without an ever-present sense of death life is insipid. You might as well live on the whites of eggs.

That seemed rather obsessive, reading books a second time and a third, as if one's memory was defective.

Henry Castlemaine loved his daughter dearly, and himself a little more.

It didn't occur to me, then, that the vertiginous blurb that was written to me about the girl was in fact so excessive as to be suspicious.

It's strange how you think you know people, and then they do something odd, and you have to start on virgin ground again.

Truth is not literally true. Truth is never the whole truth. Nothing but the truth is always a lie. The world is ours; it is in metaphorical terms our capital ... Never, never, touch the capital. Live on the interest, not on the capital. The world is ours to conserve and ours are the fruits thereof to consume. We should never consume the capital, ever. If we do, we are left with the barren and literal truth.

Neurotics are awfully quick to notice other people's mentalities, everyone goes into an exaggerated category.

What's bred in the bone comes out.

I did not remove my glasses, for I had not asked for her company in the first place, and there is a limit to what one can listen to with the naked eye.

People in those parts are very typical of each other, as one group of standing stones in that wilderness is like the next.

"Neurotics never go mad," my friends had always told me. Now I realized the distinction between neurosis and madness, and in my agitation I half-envied the woman beyond my bedroom wall, the sheer cool sanity of her behavior within the limits of her impracticable mania. Only the very mad, I thought, can come out with the information "The Lord is risen," in the same factual way as one might say, "You are wanted on the telephone," regardless of the time and place.

The superstition of today is the science of yesterday.

People, even one's friends, do go off with things. But their main objects of acquisition are books. Guests go off with books out of the guest-room.

Parents learn a lot from their children about coping with life. It is possible for parents to be corrupted or improved by their children.

Wonderful to have a whole day unplanned. It's like a blank sheet of paper to be filled in according to inspiration.

I reject the idea that it is best to have never been born.

To teach a cat to play ping-pong you have to first win the confidence and approval of the cat.

Once you know some facts about a person you are in some way involved with them.

It is always the same with people who make a fetish of self-control: they strike the most histrionic attitudes.

I chucked the antinomian pose when I was twenty. There's no such thing as a private morality.

For though he knew the general axiom that death was everyone's lot he could never realize the particular case; each new death gave him something fresh to feel.

But charity elevates the mind and governs the inward eye. If a valuable work of art is rediscovered after it has gone out of fashion, that is due to some charity in the discoverer, I believe.

There's a dirty swine in every man.

"All human beings who breathe are a bit unnatural," Dougal said. "If you try to be too natural, see where it gets you."

We all have a fatal flaw.

If there is one thing a bachelor does not like it is another bachelor who has lost his job.

It is better, (he thought) to be a pessimist in life, it makes life endurable. The slightest optimism invites disappointment.

"I'm not lonely before they come. I'm only lonely when they go away."

But safety does not come first. Goodness, Truth, and Beauty come first.

Long ago in 1945 all the nice people in England were poor, allowing for exceptions....
   All the nice people were poor; at least, that was the general axiom, the best of the rich being poor in spirit. There was absolutely no point in feeling depressed about the scene, it would have been like feeling depressed about the Grand Canyon or some event of the earth outside everybody's scope.

Nothing reveals a secret sweetness so much as a personal point of misery bursting out of a phlegmatic creature.

Why couldn't people be moderate?

And, of course, the question answered itself: she had been too memorable to remember.

It's an act of presence ... as when you visit a bereaved friend and there's nothing to say. The whole point is, that a meeting has materialized.

She had observed before that when people were in process of moving in to a new house, and until the furniture had arrived and been put in place, everyone felt they could come and go, like the workmen and the removal men, without permission.

Her talent, he thought, is a rich one. As in life, he thought, it is the very rich who understand thrift while the poor spend quickly on trifles.

When you say a thing is not impossible, that isn't quite as if to say it's possible.... Only technically is the not impossible, possible.

One who has never observed a strict ordering of the heart can never exercise freedom.

A rebellion against a tyrant is only immoral when it hasn't got a chance.

Anxiety is for the bourgeoisie and for great artists in those hours when they are neither asleep
nor practicing their art. An aristocratic soul feels
no anxiety nor, I think, do the famine-stricken
of the world as they endure the impotent ex-
tremities of starvation.

We are leaving the sphere of history and are
about to enter that of mythology. Mythology
is nothing more than history garbled; likewise
history is mythology garbled and it is nothing
more in all the history of man. Who are we to
alter the nature of things?

Masses of old, old letters are very upsetting to
contemplate, each one containing a world of
past trivialities or passions forever pending. The
surprise of words once overlooked and mean-
ings newly realized, the record of debts unpaid
or overpaid, of boredom unrequited or sweetness forever lost.

A secretary is one who keeps secrets.

A wonderful woman, a wonderful woman. She doesn't need money to make her a wonderful woman. It's only that she's used to it.

In reality, no farmer prays for rain unless the rain is long overdue; and if a miracle of good fortune occurs it is always at the moment of grace unthought-of and when everybody is looking the other way.

He was unaware that the same story that can repel can also enchant, according to the listener.

That afternoon she stepped out with the courage of her wild convictions and the dissatisfaction that has no name.

His snobbery was immense. But there was a sense in which he was far too democratic for the likes of me. He sincerely believed that talent, although not equally distributed by nature, could be later conferred by a title or acquired by inherited rank. As for memoirs they could be written, invented, by any number of ghost writers. I suspect he really believed that the Wedgwood cup from which he daintily sipped his tea derived its value from the fact that the social system had recognized the Wedgwood family, not from the china that they had exerted themselves to make.

Weakness of character: to my mind this is no more to be despised than is physical weakness. We are not all born heroes and athletes. At the same time it is elementary wisdom always to fear weaknesses, including one's own; the reactions of the weak, when touched off, can be horrible and sudden.

People who want justice generally want so little when it comes to the actuality. There is more to be had from the world than a balancing of accounts.

Another maxim was All is not Gold that Glisters, and another was Honesty is the Best Policy, and I also recall Discretion is the Better Part of Valor. And I have to testify that these precepts, which I was too flighty-minded to actually ponder at the time, but around which I dutifully curled my cursive Ps and my Vs, have turned out to my astonishment to be absolutely true. They may lack the grandeur of the Ten Commandments but they are more to the point.

The apologies of the rich. They are cheap.

The young are very generous.

"The prohibitive price of fares," said his aunt, as one multi-millionaire to another.

Lucan besides was a silk purse, and it was useless to expect such an object to turn into something so good, so true, as a sow's ear.

All obsessed gamblers are liars.

"I was given your name by an old school friend of yours in Paris."

This is a tactic in the con-business that usually works. The mention of a school friend one doesn't remember generally gives rise to a slight feeling of guilt rather than suspicion.

"The nature of jealousy ... the feeling as a sort of admiration ... to want what others had ... What is jealousy? Jealousy is to say, what you have got is mine, it is mine, it is mine? Not quite. It is to say, I hate you because you have got what I have not got and desire. I want to be me, myself, but in your position, with your opportunities, your fascination, your looks, your abilities, your spiritual good."

Proximity to a man who does nothing gets on one's nerves after a time.

A Few Last Words of Advice

There is a time for loyalty and a time when loyalty comes to an end.

And it is my advice, when you have to refuse any request that admits of no argument, you should never give reasons or set out your objections; to do so leads to counter-reasons and counter-objections.

Inevitably, I came out with my experience that very afternoon with my agent, showing her how he had flicked my typescript at me with his thumb and third finger. She took at intense interest in the story. "My dear," she said, "you must acquire a pair of lorgnettes, make an occasion to see that man again, focus the glasses on him and sit looking at him through them as if he was an insect. Just look and look."

There is a lot of nasty stuff in life which comes breaking up our ecstasy, our inheritance. People should read more poetry and dream their dreams.

If you imagine that appearance may belie the reality, then you are wrong. Appearances are reality.

You should never take guidance from one man only. From many men, many women, yes, by watching them and hearing, and finally consulting with yourself. It's the only way. Life should be one's guidance director.

One should see a psychiatrist only out of boredom.

Be on the alert to recognize your prime at whatever time of your life it may occur.

"Mustn't come between husband and wife," he said. "Inadvisable. You get no thanks, and they both turn on you."

Dangerous people often seem boring.

My advice to any woman who earns the reputation of being capable, is to not demonstrate her ability too much. You give advice; you say, do this, do that, I think I've got you a job, don't worry, leave it to me. All that, and in the end you feel spooky, empty, haunted. And if you then want to wriggle out of so much responsibility, the people around you are outraged. You have stepped out of your role. It makes them furious.

For my part, it's not that I don't suffer fools gladly, but that I don't suffer them at all.

"Try again tomorrow." "One never knows. Life is like a lottery."

It was a bungle like any other bungle. You should never let a bungle weigh on your conscience.

Knots were not necessarily created to be untied. Questions were things that sufficed in their still beauty, answering themselves.

Frankness is usually a euphemism for rudeness.

"On the question of will-power, if that is a factor, you should think of will-power as something that never exists in the present tense, only in the future and the past. At one moment you have decided to do or refrain from an action and the next moment you have already done or refrained; it is the only way to deal with will-power. (Only under sub-human stress does will-power live in time present but that is a different discourse.) I offer this advice without fee; it is included in the price of this book."